THE HOUSE OF PUNISHMENT

THE HOUSE OF PUNISHMENT

Dedication, Determination and Desire . . .

Editorials & Poems Written

by

D E E   ' L Y N N E

iUniverse, Inc.
Bloomington

THE HOUSE OF PUNISHMENT

iUniverse books may be ordered through booksellers or by contacting:

iUniverse
1663 Liberty Drive
Bloomington, IN 47403
www.iuniverse.com
1-800-Authors (1-800-288-4677)

ISBN: 978-1-4697-9579-9 (sc)
ISBN: 978-1-4697-9580-5 (hc)
ISBN: 978-1-4697-9581-2 (ebk)

Printed in the United States of America

iUniverse rev. date: 05/02/2012

TABLE OF CONTENTS

Chapter Six

ABOUT THE AUTHOR

Dee 'Lynne is a High School graduate, major course was business, I am a dedicated, loyal and a lovable woman; I have a passion for teaching. I had many careers in my lifetime caring for children and adults. I am now achieving my (CDA) Child Development Associate Credential in Early Childhood Development, as a childcare practitioner educator; I will continue to grow using resources with other organizations pertaining to this field such as (NAEYC) National Association for the Education of Young Children, my home is in Philadelphia Pennsylvania.

DEDICATION

This book is to family and friends, those who are here physically, and those who are in my heart. I like to thank my two sons who in their own way brought experiences and lessons to be learned in my life, it help me stay focus and they help me to be who I am today, You are my motivation and inspiration.

The brother who is doing the time, but not letting the time do him, I dedicate this book on behalf of your strengths, efforts and courage, I am here for you physically, mentally, spiritually and emotionally, you always will have a shoulder to lean on.

In memory of my father and my mother it was from your seed I was produce and I honor that.

*My sisters and brothers who had a listening ear, whenever I needed someone to **talk, laugh, cry, and holler with**, thank you.*

And last my friends, those that stayed on me faithfully, I commend you for your time and the faith you have in me, and most of all I would like to **shout-out peace-out.**

ACKNOWLEDGEMENT

It was a beautiful evening for me; I was at home alone that Friday evening, with thoughts of the day, wondering through my mind. With my idol time I decided to do something different, I didn't want to watch television, I had no plans to go anywhere this particular night, so I sat back and gather my thoughts together. Before I knew it I was at my computer typing.

I am the type of person who prays over ever situation, not knowing the outcomes, but I do believe that there is a GOD. It takes time, effort and motivation, along with an open-mind and wiliness to believe in our dreams. So I prayed and I asked GOD to help me through the journey that I am about to take.

Cedar Point, Ohio, living in a household of twelve siblings, in which both parents are now still together. Well life was not easy, but sometimes very complicated. There was so much to be learned and had to be done as children, living in this world of society. With all types of different personalities, within the family, it was hard to ever hear I love you, from any of the family members, including the parents, seems like the word love was against the law.

My mother Charlotte was an ordinary housewife, who stood by her husband, Charles, no matter if he was right or wrong. Both of my parents were very strict, my father, you could forget trying to pull the wool over his eyes, or face.

There was a lot of favoritism within this family; I could remember some of the things back in the sixty and seventies. Even into the years of the eighties, there was not much crime known of back then. It took a village to raise a child, everybody mother, was everybody mother. If you were caught in the act by another parent, or teacher, anyone with authority, they had the right to punish you, and then take you home to your parents, for the rest of the disciplining. Back then in the sixties, do the math, I was young and very knowledgeable.

I had the responsibilities, of taking care of my younger six siblings. Remember, I am the seventh child from the youngest of twelve siblings. Charles would say Lynne, go on out, and take your sisters and brothers with you, I would like you all to stay in the front of the building, where I can see you. Mind you we did live in the Projects; there are so many names for these high-rise buildings. They were thirteen stories high; we lived on the lobby floor of this building.

Our windows went from the front of the building all the way around to the sides. Therefore my dad was always in a window. There were five siblings older than myself, of course they had rules to follow, and their life was just as complicated as the younger ones. I always felt that I was the black sheep of the family, teased a lot and over-looked. I was a very, very thin child, but I also had a good sense of humor, I took the sweet with the bad.

I did have common sense about some of the things in which I have seen in my life, I did not much understand a lot of it, maybe it was too much for me to know as a child, that is where the mistake began, in my life. Some things are important for your children to know, about life, the street, sex, drugs, gangs, and so much more involved, I can say part of this caused my situation to change either for the better or the worse.

There were times when I found myself, very rebellious against my father, I would always confront him as though I was the parent, I thought I was doing the right thing, whenever I thought my dad was wrong when approaching one of my siblings I would defend them, and this I could not understand, why I would take the fall. If you ask me I say it was out of love. Or maybe I thought there was a better way, I could remember times on my way to school, or coming home from school, I would find money, and run home to tell my parents, just for them to take the money out of my hands to use for their own purposes.

At times during the summer whenever the Ice-cream truck would show up, Charles would then have everybody line up oldest to youngest? There were other times Charles would take us to the park, and have to make a second trip, for the other siblings. It just seems to me while growing up, every weekend, either my mother side of the family would, be over or my father side of his family would visit.

Those was the good old days, we did get to know some of our relatives. Also remember when I was in the fourth grade, and I had a crush on this boy name Joseph Browner. I would wear this one hair style, my hair was pretty thick and long, natural, a part down the middle of my head and two puff-balls on each side. Well Joseph liked my hair this way, and every time my mother was ready to redo my hair I would have a fit.

I guessed as time went on, my parents were getting older in age. I know for sure I don't remember either one of them, or the two of them sitting me down and talking to me about sex, explaining what the outcomes will lead me too. There were a lot of secrets in my family, which just, were not supposed to be known. I could never understand, why my father Charles, would raise us up on a lie.

There were certain situations, in which a child should not know, but this, made me not know who I was for a long time, including not knowing the personalities of my siblings. Which broke the bond between us, and as I speak we are so far apart, it broke the bond of communication, the love and the unity, that we do not have not have for each other today. Charles had his favorite ones, and as much denial that Charlotte was in, she went right along, with everything Charles said or did. I could not tell whether my mother and father, were ever in love during my childhood.

There just was not enough love going around in our household. That hurt me a lot, because as I said before, I always felt like the black sheep. Even though I gotten older, I some time still do. Charles was a hard working man, he did provide for our family. Charlotte whenever she was not giving birth to another child, she would work part-time, when all the children attended school.

Living in the high-rise, projects, whatever you would like to call them, there were many big families living in these high-rise buildings, there were a lot of card games going on, bingo night out, or just hanging in another adult apartment drinking, and having fun. The different between now and then is, that the rate of crime was unacceptable. You could walk out of your apartment and leave the doors unlock and the windows open.

If you were living in a house, you could leave the door wide open, and expect no harm to come your way. The crimes that were committed, back in the fifties-eighties were a slap on the wrist and hand, miscellaneous mishaps. Mostly committed by young adolescents, as they were doing stupid things such as starting a riot, just to break into department stores, even busting out car windows, or running away from home, underage drinking. You know the typical sinner kind of things. When getting themselves into some fist fights, this brought about the Police Officers.

But these crimes were taken care of fair, and square. Now living in the world of today society, all havoc broke loose. You have crimes that have been committed, and because you are from a poor family, and you are an African-American, not by choice, but through society, you have already lost the battle. The crimes that are committed today are very breath taking and the capacity of love, that one should have for themselves they should have for others.

What possibly went wrong, GOD gave each and every one of us as human being, the greatest, most precious gift any one could ever, ask for LIFE and what came with the gift were choices, to know right from wrong. You must be careful how you live your life, what you make of your life. No matter what, there is a price to pay, whether good or bad. It is like a book the choices you make are the outline of your life.

I have found myself in many different situations, where it came about a struggle, easy as heck getting into something, but hard as heck, wanting out. You must be careful in whatever you say or do, what goes around does come around. My story is based on People or a Person, who committed a crime, you wonder what triggers, a person's behavior, or their way of thinking to commit such violence. Do most of these situations start from home base?

To tell the truth, speaking for myself, I believe that the situation of a human being, thoughts and actions, play a great deal of their childhood lifestyle. Growing up from childhood, it is very important as a parent, or parents, to talk to your children, as well as listen to whatever they have to say. I can think back, and look at my life experiences today, and say my childhood, without the knowledge of GOD our creator, and his good will, I would have benefited from fulfilling my dreams.

Also from experience with having children of my own, I took a lot from their lives; I should have really been there when they needed me. I could have put aside all the partying, having fun, meeting different guys or whatever the circumstances were. The main important issues were the children lives. If you ever focus, or just thought, when you were alone, about certain things, you did and went through during your childhood, whether good or bad, and where you are now in life, it is a retrace of your past.

Whatever you set your mind to do, as we are now mature adults, knowing right from wrong, these were our choices, which now affect our future.

Believe me, when I tell you this, if I could do it all over again, it would be done quite differently. See what I am saying is my experience of my life, which helps me to talk about someone else life, who I have know for a long time. Crime, Crimes, Crimes, will they ever end? It will truly take prayers from the people of this world, to bring upon a miracle. I thank GOD, and my Lord and Savior Christ Jesus, for the grace and mercy which is upon us.

ADMITTANCE

MY BRAIN IS FINALLY AT EASE, I CAN FINALLY BREATHE
RECOVERING FROM THIS HORRIBLE DISEASE, NO MORE DRUGS PLEASE
TIME TO TAKE HEED TO ALL MY NEEDS, MY DESPERATION BLEEDS
MY HEART IS TRAPPED IN VICE GRIPS, IN A TIGHT SQUEEZE
THE PAIN SECRETES THROUGH MY PORES, I NEED TO HEAL THESE RESENTFUL SORES
I DON'T WANNA HURT NO MORE, DROP THE FALSE PRESENTATION AT THE DOOR
SEARCHING FOR A GUIDING LIGHT, TO LEAD ME TO A FUTURE THAT SHINES BRIGHT,
AWAY FROM THE PAST LIFE.

IN A PRESENT TIME OF ALL THAT'S RIGHT, SO I CAN PAY IT FORWARD, BY LIVING
TOWARDS IT, LENDING A HELPING HAND TO THE NEXT HUMAN
WHILE TAKIN A STAND FOR OUR CHILDREN'S, WHO ARE FEELING AND DEALING
REACH OUT, SPEAK AT, LIVE OUT LOUD, THE MIST OF LIFE RAINS DOWN ON US
IF YOU DOWN THEN, WHY NOT JOIN US.

INTRODUCTION

I am blessed in so many ways, I judge no one, for the crimes, that they commit, I only know, in my heart, somewhere in these person inner thoughts, they are crying out for help. In some way that, they cannot even identify. I realize things happen for a reason, but in such cases, like rape, murder, or committing suicide, that is insanity.

You get caught up in the mix of trying to be like someone else, or not knowing, who you are, could be part of the game that we play. In most cases, 50% of these crimes are drug-related and the other 50% can just be from holding onto the past, for such a long time and never talking to anyone about your inner thoughts or feeling, which can be very detrimental. As I defined the words, Denial refusing to admit reality as unpleasant. Anger, an easy cover up for a feeling that is uncomfortable, such as fear, hurt, and guilt. All human beings have ways of protecting ourselves against what we see and or feel as danger. No matter what situation we are dealing with, WE HAVE MET THE ENEMY, AND HE IS YOU. So I came to learn to love myself, for who I am, and the things that I will accomplish in my life. I must first deal with any dirt from my past, clean up the mess. Analyze what got me where I am in the first place. Live life to the fullest, especially, after you had several chances to improve ourselves. No one said life would be easy, but it is what you make of it.

You make your bed, you lie in it, like I said, and these are some of my thoughts and most of my experiences. I can just about know and explain my feelings, as I can observe what is around me. It does not take a scientist to write a book; just say what is on your mind, and what is in your heart. Still we as human beings need to know our purpose of being here. The crimes that are being committed, the rates are so high I feel for the Police Officers, Doctors, and the Firemen, not even mentioning the Judges and so on, they are on call twenty-four seven. How must their families feel, it has to be very devastating on them.

Well I had to let you in on something about myself the (author) the beginning and the end it should be a very unique outcome, to any human being that has been through or who is dealing with such a situation, with someone so close to them, whether a family member or just a friend, who may have lost all hope along their way, by not believing in a power greater then themselves. My prayers goes out to you and your love ones, in whatever crimes they made have committed, that they have peace, love, and hope, if they should have to do life in prison. May GOD and his Angels be upon them, that they may accept the responsibilities, of their actions, and come to a complete understanding of acceptance, that their pain can be no greater than to whom it was done to, while it was being done? In Jesus Christ name I pray. (Amen)

NEVER BACK DOWN

TO THE NEGATIVE ENERGY IN AND OUTSIDE THESE WALLS,
NEVER LET THEM MAKE YOU FALL.
FOR THOSE WHO SAID IT CAN'T BE DONE, YOU MUST NOT KNOW THAT I AM THE ONE
THEY SHOULD NOT INTERRUPT THOSE WHO ARE DOING IT,
IT TAKES MORE ENERGY BEING MAD, RATHER THAN BEING GLAD
MISERY LOVES COMPANY, KEEP IN MIND WHO YOU KEEP COMPANY WITH DON'T WORRY BE
HAPPY, LET NO ONE STEAL YOUR

JOY!

Chapter One

THE DEFENDANT

I believed if we were told the truth from the beginning of time, the way **GOD** had wanted it to be, this might have been a better place to live. There are different walks of life, race, creed, and color, but who put the decisions in our hand, as being a Judge, Doctor, Police Officer, or even a Lawyer.

Well let me take the time to tell you a story, which is detrimental, painful and touching. As far as I can remember I have always wanted to write about something dealing with reality, as long as the story made sense and those who would read it not only enjoyed reading the story but also understood the writer point of view.

There comes a time and place in everyone's life, when we might not admit to our mistakes. Though mistakes can be erased but they will never go away. With such high crime going on in this world today, things are happening all around us so fast. You sometimes wonder if the Judge or the Prosecutor and even the Lawyer really have the time to analyze the situations. In many circumstances they may just throw away the key with the knowledge of knowing the truth of the matter pertaining to the crime. In this story there are many people who play a great part. The defendant who is

1

helpless to the crime, he comes from a very large and poor family. A family that cares about him, and love him, but not enough to put forth the effort to seeing that something is done, to help him through his state of depression, lack of faith, loneliness, pride and dignity, as a human being. The ways that real families are suppose to be, bonded, loving, supportive, and understanding.

I know how it feels being brought up in a large family, with confusion, and lies. Making that turn around the corner or walking down the wrong street. That second, minute, or hour that something detrimental happens you feel alone, when you really need your family where are they now? Were they always there before this crime was committed? It would make me think twice if I was in this situation.

Here we have a defendant who is not only alone, scared, confused, but who also was a drug addict. Who lost all hopes and dreams along his road of trial and tribulations? During his High School Years, peer pressures play a big part in his life, all focus pertaining to the subjects didn't matter anymore, and somewhere, somehow, and he lost sight of his purpose for being here on this earth.

Why am I here? What are my accomplishments? What are God plans for me? Some people just don't take the time to know who they are. Don't have a clue.

Anyway during the hard time of this young man's life he lost his father, somewhat around the beginning of his addiction. Therefore his role model no longer existed. He was oldest of his baby brother, but had quite few others older than he. What good were they to Royale, when they too had problems to face? Most who have left home anyway. Some of the other siblings just didn't have the time.

Never not one time thinking, or saying by the Grace of God there goes I. You can always remember getting there, the hard part is not knowing how, and never forgetting where you come from. During the time that Royale, committed these crimes he was deeply and so involved with drugs, and alcohol, there was no light to see his way though. Royale did many things to try and kick the habit, just didn't know how to stop.

He would always say Lynne it is so easy to do badly, but it is hard as heck trying to do what is right. I could remember times he would tell me just don't buy the drugs and you won't get high. What I am saying is reality because I do play a big part in my brother life. As said I am my brother keeper. Times have been hard throughout Royale life. Like any human being he's has to pay the price for a crime that he committed.

How is that without a fair trial? Misled by the Jury, Judge, Prosecutor and somewhat Public Defender, Royale is a loving and caring person, who has been a victim of drug abuse. Not knowing where to turn in any situation with guidance can be hard. Crying out for help from the inside as a child when your own parents wouldn't listen to your cries is very unbearable. Not ever hearing that I love you, or telling you I am proud of you, everything is going to be alright. I'm here for you if you need someone to talk to. Royale didn't know where drugs would lead him to.

It all started out to be pleasure and fun, uncontrollable as time passed by. Only it was too late when he proceeded under the influence of drugs and alcohol. My brother who is very intelligent, his choices of words are touching, he speaks with such knowledge. We as God children's were put on this earth for purposes, crimes should have never played a part in anyone's life. God has mercy on Royal.

For if he had another chance for a fair hearing I believe Royale could defend himself. The system knows what really happen, the cause of nature pertaining to these crimes but as told before Royale was railroaded. For the crimes that he had committed is just unexplainable. The peoples who were at the scene of the crime, at the hospital, during the time of his apprehension, in the courtroom, the room that the jury makes their decisions in all plays a big part in this cover up.

I pray for Royale, each and every day of our lives, I just keep on thinking about the night that this incident took place. I will never forget it as long as I live. That same night had I know what his intentions were maybe, they could have been prevented. I struggle with the pain that Royale carries inside. The strangest thing about families there's suppose to be enough love to go around, where did it go wrong. I believe if we were raised a little better, and told the truth of how to love one another, be there for each other no matter what, our faith would be much stronger. Don't get me wrong our parents provided for us to the best of their abilities. Never seen a hungry day went to school every day, something was missing.

Favoritism played a great deal in or lives. I am the black sheep of the family and so was Royale. There were many of times that we were over looked, no matter what I was still there to love my family in the best way I knew how too. I just wished my family was closer. Royale habit became very distraught and dysfunctional, there were times he would do things not intentionally, but he caused pain towards the family, which that still doesn't make him less human.

You do not have to be on drugs to understand someone's reaction. If you learned that person you would know the different behaviors that come from within that particular human being. If I knew what I know now maybe a miracle could have been performed. He did many things that were not very pleasurable to talk about, but who am I to judge. I do know that as a child Royale was a very sane person.

Even though our parents told us right from wrong, it's this wall that we build around us, wanting to find out the hard way on our own. Very vicious circles that just go round and round and round, bumping your head on every corner that you turn. What does it take to have a rude awakening, or even hit rock bottom. Royale hit his bottom pretty hard, but yet his rude awakening is even harder to deal with. I believe that he has not come to accepting the responsibilities of his time in prison. It all happened so fast. Just one day you free as a bird, but in this case using drugs, you are never free. Royale was already a prison in his own mind.

He didn't know how to maintain the subconscious mind that he lived with each and every day of his addiction. He fell weak to his own thoughts and intuitions, he acted out on impulses, and maybe thinking again this time I get away with whatever action I would perform. As a drug addict getting high was the only thing he knew, with no job, no hustle, what else was there to do. Waking up wanting to get high, going to bed if you found the time to, **No** moral thoughts, no dignity, and no respect for yourself or anyone else.

Royale lost all feeling inside he didn't know the meaning of love anymore. Therefore he took upon himself desperate measure. Any means necessarily. When a crime is committed under the influence of drugs and alcohol is there no legal alternative for such behaviors? I feel that I need to help my brother Royale to tell his story; this is my way of showing that I love him.

You know even though Royale is incarcerated he still has the love and concern for his family, and he's only one person. There's not much he can do for himself serving life in prison. Each and every time that I read one of his letters or hear from him through telecommunication I felt the need for strength and encouragement to move forward and to keep the focus on the more important things in life. Royale tries to be strong, his saying, don't even break a sweat worrying about me. That's very impossible to do, he is my brother, a part of me my flesh and blood we are one. Don't get me wrong Royale does have his down days went his spirit is broken, that because he feels so alone at times. I really feel for him.

This is a blessing from above; I thank God that my brother is still alive. The life that he was living during his addiction, he was spared then, by the almighty Creator, the only thing we don't know, if we can't feel it, or see it, but he is there. Let me tell you something, and, that is that, every good thing comes from above. I lift this situation up in prayer.

Royale continue caring about everyone in his family on the outside, why not do the same for him. Now during this time of Royal incarceration, he was able to find a case exactly like his, and in a shadow of a doubt that case was dismissed. Afterward knowing this Royale tried to get legal help pertaining to this matter, but again his was being overlooked. Royale has been incarcerated for quite some time now.

The only trial that he had was the first one which sentences him to life in prison. With several others counts which were not justified in the court of law. During the time of my brother sentence it had to be like a nightmare, only he was awaken to witness his own trial. The bad part of this he had no family there for support. Very distraught from the night before after the use of drugs and alcohol waking up not even realizing where you are. What Royale did, he would have never done in his entire life if he had been sane. Should there had been an evaluation done on this addict, could he had needed Psychological Moment.

How can you really be tried for a crime that is committed under the influence of drugs and alcohol? It is a mental sickness as well as a crying shame. Royale mom was on her sick bed, four years after his incarceration, he blamed himself for that. He carried so much grieves inside of his mind and body he wanted to die. He wasn't able to be there to make his amends, or to attend the funeral it took a great toil on his heart.

Did the system care anything about the situation? Royale wrote me telling me that he had a Public Defender the Court Office hire for him, but still no fair hearing was ever brought about. He kept his hopes up saying, when the court assign me a date for another trial, he would let me know, but still no fair hearing ever came about. It has now been nine years, what is the hold up with this case. I tell you it is a cover-up.

During the time of the victim's incident something went very wrong with one of the patients while hospitalized. It has to have been very hard to be in a State Penitentiary amongst different walks of life. Royale wasn't out to hurt anyone that night, along with killing someone, just another addict with a habit. His prime purpose was to try and get whatever he could, money, jewelry, appliances, whatever the nature called for, but not to hurt anyone. Instead not knowing that one of the victims, who was elderly, and sickly? Royale just wanted in and out. Still under the influence of drugs and alcohol, he reacted off of his impulses.

He brought about trauma to the victims, especially the husband who then was hospitalized that same night. Now as I know this patient was already on Coumadin (Warfarin Sodium) a blood thinner. Coumadin can also result to death. Intracranial hemorrhage that is grouped with the major bleeding. All other things pertaining to this case will come about. You know how when you can feel in your heart when something isn't right, well Royale has the same spirit feeling in his heart.

He takes full responsibility for all other actions, this one was put on him, and it was proven in his trial. Both Royale and I ask and pray to God that this case be revealed again so that his innocence is proven. Royale is putting so much energy into proving his innocence he had finally gotten briefs together to send to the Public Defender Office, the Prosecutor Office and the County Clerk.

It is really hard when you're not getting the proper help that is needed. There was also a case that Royale gotten a hold of, that stated a car accident, this man died, and his wife was trying to collect from the Insurance Company saying the accident killed her husband, but the Insurance Company said the accident didn't kill him. It was the anticoagulation "Warfarin" Coumadin and he died from a blood clot in his head. Same thing happened in Royale case, a patient who was on "Warfarin" Coumadin. Now the ruling on that case by the Court was that the accident was not the cause of death, by the evidence, it was the Warfarin that brought forth the death. And then they go on to say that even if there was some relationship between the accident and the death, the accident was not the sole cause of death, the Warfarin still was the contributing factor which brought forth the death.

Some things happen and peoples just tend to look the other way. We are dealing with a human being life; the truth shall set us free. Most of the letters that I received from Royale are all stating, he still waiting for an appeal. Then came about a letter saying he finally had another court date July 2003. But to tell the truth I don't remember if it ever came to pass, it just to get Royale to stop writing the Judge. Royale does have enough evidence to prove his innocence, and their wrong-doings that happen in court.

This is a very hard and distinctive case. Royale has been strong to this point, but what is a man to do in his situation, when he has no outside help. Serving time in prison at the same time playing around with a human being life, not giving the benefit of the doubt what becomes of this nature. Time is of essence and not to be wasted. Royale is paying for these crimes that were committed, but what is he really paying for, someone else mistake that is being covered-up by false accusations. At the same time those who performed such preliminary actions, are living their lives as though nothing ever happen during the time of the incident, to the victim during his hospitalization. If there was to be another trial, for the defendant things will become different for him in his case.

To observe this case the Attorney will have to be very open-minded, and focus to see that that the defendant has been misled. All the facts are in black and white, how much more is there to say in such a manner of circumstances that leads many people's right to the evidence. I know that this is happening all around the world to many people, yes that have committed a crime, but is paying the price for someone else mistake. This is where it doesn't end.

Something must be done for many cases like this defendant. There is not point of return for Royale without the right legal actions. How someone like the defendant will serve life in prison, without parole, very obscure, never ever having another trial while serving his time in a State Penitentiary know the innocent of his crimes. Telling his side of the story to the arresting Officers after waiving his rights and agreed to give a statement only if the detective put down what he said.

If he did not, the defendant would be allowed to ripping up the statement. The detective agreed to defendant stipulation. Defendant then gave the following statement: he got into the building because the tenant buzzed him in; he knocked on the door and when he opened the door and went inside, an assault and robbery followed. The defendant further stated: he did not force his way into the apartment. The door was opened by the female victim. The assault took place in the living room, defendant then stated that he used his hands to commit the assault and that his assault caused one victim to fall to the floor; that he then took two gold watches.

At the end of his statement, defendant added that he "wished to plead insanity," that he wanted to talk to someone who dealt with "this stuff," and that there was a lot of pressure in his head" he could not deal with because of some injuries he had sustained as a result of an unrelated incident. Although he failed to move for a new trial before the trial court as required, the defendant nonetheless claims, for the first time on appeal., that his conviction for felony murder should be set aside because the State's evidence was insufficient to establish that the victim's death was a probable consequence of his conduct, and the defendant should have, had the rights to professional care, as stated in his comments to be evaluated by a psychologist, in dealing with his emotions, behaviors, and state of mind.

One of the saddest part of this whole concept is that the defendant did not have much support from his family pertaining to legal representation. During his time of sentencing feeling alone, barely seeing and thinking clearly, no moral support, not knowing where it will end, lost, and misguided, no character witness to speak in good turn for this young man. His lost his only chance to raise the issue in the trial court; he is barred from doing so now, for the first time on appeal.

There was many, many issue that was over-looked pertaining to the defendant rights; the defendant must now demonstrate that the omission of the charge constituted plain error that is error of such magnitude as "clearly capable of producing an unjust result." Otherwise the omission shall be disregarded. In this case any or everything that the defendant says is merit less. The energy it takes to hide and pretend is the energy you need to live your life and move on.

Being incarcerated and doing life in prison, withdraws so much energy, from your mind, body, and spirit, where this would led the defendant too. Would the defendant be rehabilitated, what does a prison offer an inmate, which is serving life in prison without parole? Knowing that this defendant could not reach out to the peoples who he loved the most. Trying to get outside resources, from family members, who were more informed of getting the information that he requires.

It is a very painful situation, especially during the time of visiting days, you're sitting there in the television room, or maybe in your cell, just wondering, and maybe today someone will come and see me. It truly is a bad situation that the defendant put his self in, but with the love and strength from his family, this can help make him strong physically and mentally while serving his time in a penitentiary.

It's no easy way of doing time in any penitentiary, but the time that has been served by the defendant, one good positive outlook was achieved. Which is the defendant now has his sanity back, from the use of drugs and alcohol. From this point forward everything is dealing with reality. He has free himself from the abusive world of insanity; at this point he does know that he is responsible for his actions. Royale is more than willing to do his time, but he is dealing with several charges that could have been merged into one charge. It is as though his life was thrown away, he doesn't even have an Attorney (public defender) that comes by to talk about his case.

He was incarcerated and whatever happens afterward, whether he beaten down, locked down, raped, sick from something that he has eaten, is there anyone in the system that cares. His family surely wouldn't know, because they don't even pay him a visit, not as much as writing, him. That I couldn't understand. How much time does it take to say I love you, or I am here for you, it doesn't cost you a thing? You may hear quite a few times, oh I hate writing, I never like writing, I couldn't find the time I'm so busy.

How can you not find the time for your love ones. Only when you as a person can be responsible with the welfare of everyone involved in mind can a family move toward healing. Anyone who has been though something like this should talk about it. Instead in some sense the defendant no longer exists, he's in another time frame, of his own world, locked down, forgotten, where he came from and where he is now.

11

Yes the defendant has to pay for his crime and he must do the time, you surely cannot go back and change anything; however in another court of law, with the defendant case being evaluated in the prospected manner, the situation would have been looked at differently, these chances are against the odds, serving his time in a penitentiary.

This would at least help the defendant know what his outcomes are. At this point and time every charge that has been brought against the defendant is so unbearable to handle, he is ready to unfold, to clean up his mess, but yet, with a new attitude and the knowledge he possesses, bring hope and knowledge upon his lesson.

Have he forgiven himself, it is a bad experience when someone else life is involved, and you as the defendant play a great part of this crime, not intending, for anything to go wrong or get out of hand. You may wonder what was going through his subconscious mind, while still today he lies in his cell paying the price of a human life.

A CLEAN REALIZATION

HOW MANY OF US HAVE BEEN KING FOR A DAY, JUST GOT PAID AND WANTED TO PLAY MOST OF Y'ALL KNOW WHAT I MEAN, WE PLAYED THE SAME COURT, JUST DIFFERENT TEAMS. WHEN YOU THAT DUDE CALLING THE SHOTS, WITH A KNOT OF MONEY, AND TONS OF ROCK, LIIVING IT UP FOR JUST A MINUTE, NOT GIVEN A CHANCE, CAUSE YOU WERENT FINISHED.

WHEN IT'S ALL GONE AND DONE, YOU THEN REALIZE SO IS EVERYONE.
WHEN YOUR POCKETS, ARE FAT, EVERYBODY GOT CHA BACK, NOW YOUR POCKETS ARE TAPPED, CAUSED YOU DONE SMOKED A WHOLE LOT OF CRACK.

NOW YOU'RE LEFT ALONE, STUCK ON STUPID, WALKING AROUND LOST AND CLUELESS.
ON TOP OF FEELING, USELESS, YOU'RE NOW SCARED TO GO HOME AND FACE THE MUSIC.

ANCESTORS OF GREAT KING AND QUEENS, OF MANY GAVE GOOD KNOWLEDGE AND IT WAS PLENTY. I'M TRAINING TO BE ROYALTY; I WANT MY FAMILY BACK IT'S ABOUT LOYALTY.
HERE IS WHERE WE PRACTICE, DO THE THING AND LETS NOT GET TOO RELAXED.
I GOTTA NEED, I GOTTA HABIT, AND NO MORE KING FOR A DAY ITS KING FOR A LIFETIME.

I' AM WILLING TO SAVE MY LIFE, IF YOR WILLING TO THROW ME A LIFE LINE.
TAKE A BOW THE PLAY IS OVER NOW, ITS CURTAINS, GET RID OF ALL THE HURTIN DONE IT ALL, THERE IS NOTHING LEFT, TO MISS, CREATE SOME NEW GOALS, MAKE A LIST.

IF YOU NOT MY FRIEND, THEN YOU MUST BE FOE. ON THE REAL YOU GOTTA GO.
I WANT POSITIVE FRIENDS IN MY CIRCLE, I DON'T CARE IF THEIR NERDS LIKE ERCLE, I CAN LEARN FROM THEM AND MAKE IT ROUTINE, BUT I CAN ONLY ACHIEVE IT, IF I JUST STAY CLEAN.

Chapter Two

THE VICTIMS

The Pierce, who have been living in Ohio for over forty-five years, the couple whom are in their late sixty's, was a very nice and devoted couple to their community, and church, were perhaps out for dinner and a movie that night, before coming home to a quiet and relaxing night.

Living in the environment that they resided in, they were quite well known. A family of dignity and respect, innocent victims to unknown circumstances of mishaps that took place that night. While relaxing and watching television, Mrs. Pierce, heard a knock at the door. Not expecting anyone that night, she looked out the peep-hole, and asked who was there. However, she could not discern the knocker's face or the person response.

Believing it was a neighbor's brother who had come to retrieve his mail, Mrs. Pierce, unlocked the door and proceeded to open it. Before she could open the door the defendant pushed his way into the apartment. Shoving Mrs. Pierce back, he then asked where is the money.

Because most crime can happen in a home, the victims do, not leave much money in their possessions. The defendant who was under the influence of drugs and alcohol, then demanded repeatedly, where is the money. Mrs. Pierce was then assaulted by defendant. At this time the husband proceeded to raise up from his chair, defendant then knocked him to the floor. The loud noises carried out that a downstairs, neighbor, began to worry about the victims. So he called the Security Officer, of the premises, which had not responded on the first call, he then called 911.

This elderly couple, who has been, victimized into a crime of violence, distraught both the husband, and wife. It brought about fear, to this elderly couple. Mrs. Pierce and her husband were then taken to the hospital for observation, of the attack. Mr. Pierce who was already a sickly man, had suffer with such enormous health problems, in which the attacker did not acknowledge, continue the robbery and to be in and out of the apartment without hurting anyone seriously to the point of hospitalization.

The Pierce who worked all their lives and the time has come for them to retired, brought about tragedy into their life. It is a sad situation, to become a part of anyone's life, not knowing who they are and where they had come from.

What gives you the right to take actions into your own hands, when the circumstances are not to help a person but to hurt them? Later on after the Pierce had been observed by the Doctor, Mrs. Pierce was released, her husband was then sent to another hospital for tests to be performed.

Mr. Pierce who was in stable condition, had to be under severe watch. It is sad to learn that Mr. Pierce expired. There are all types of crime in this world today, death is at hand, and tomorrow is not promise. We as GOD children's do not know what is before us.

We live in a world of unknown forces. When someone you love is taken from you, not by the will of GOD but through other forces, it's hard to except. It bring about fear everywhere you go,

15

it may even have you afraid to leave the house at times. Victims are not numbered, you don't have to wait in any line, it happens by random. Each and every day of our lives something is begin planned through and evil force. It is taking place all over the world today.

As human being in the world of today we must know right from wrong, left from right, good and bad, love and hate. We are all victims, of society. Where will it led us to, and when will it all end.

There are many innocent victims throughout the world, which violence plays a big part in their lives. What does this bring about, you would think the person that is bringing harm towards, another human being, what thoughts, are on their mind. Mrs. Pierce whom has grown to love her husband, all the years that they have spent together, she now has to know how to live her life without, Mr. Pierce. It has taken some time for her to adjust, with the love of her family and friends, Mrs. Pierce decided to move in with a relative.

Hard as it is to say, it put a strenuous amount of grieving on her heart. She is paying the price for something that she had no doing. Mrs. Pierce whom in which was bruised pretty badly, during the robbery, was still shaken-up, just felt she should had been the one to die. Misled in not knowing, (why), why is the question? It is sad to say, that the world we are living in today, has become a very wicked place.

These circumstances were brought about by human being. GOD has gave us as his children's, hope, love, faith, trust, caring, and the power overall to dominate over all animals and species. The most we can do is show some respect, and gratitude. Mrs. Pierce finally decided a year and a half later, after the death of her husband.

To move into a Senior Citizen Home, where she would be more comfortable around people of her age, she had gotten to know quite a few of the people that reside in this home. Best of all she became acquainted with someone, she could finally trust in to tell her misfortune to. Afraid as Mrs. Pierce was to tell her story, almost two years later, she beginning telling her best friend Erma. Erma Stable who was also a victim of crime, has been living at this home for nearly 8 years, was attacked coming home from a doctor appointment, just three years before Mrs. Pierce tragedy occurred.

Erma which now walks with a limp was brutally attacked by three men, looking for a get high. It didn't matter the color of her skin, or the way she walked, nor did her age have anything to do with it. They wanted what they wanted, right then and there. Grabbing Erma from behind and throwing her down to the ground face down, no witnesses, or anyone to call out for help.

One of the hoodlum then cover her mouth, as the other two grab her arms behind, Erma then try to lift up, when sudden her left side was shoved to the concrete ground, they then searched her and snatch away Erma pocketbook, and told her to stay put, until they were out of sight. Shaking with such tremble, Erma had tears running down her face while telling Mrs. Pierce her story.

A part of her was destroyed, she was alone, afraid, and very scared, Erma laid on the hot ground for such a long time until finally, someone came alone and saw her, as the guy gotten closer, he couldn't believe what he was seeing, it was Erma son Teddy, on his way to visit her. Teddy in a frantic uproar, ran toward the building telling the Security Guard, call 911 my mother was just attacked.

He then picked his mother up from the ground and carries her over to the benches.

Mrs. Pierce asked Erma, how did you ever overcome this tragedy, with a gracious smile on her face, she answered, Mrs. Pierce, saying

I am grateful to still be alive, I prayed and talked to GOD, about what has happened to me that day, a few week later the same three guy's that attacked me were in a tragic stolen car accident, and very critical conditions. My prayers were answered, not that I pray for anything bad to happen to these fellows, but that they are caught before someone else becomes another victim of crime.

So as Mrs. Pierce begin to tell Erma, about her attack, she said after I tell you my story, I will say a pray so that my heart will be content. I carried this grieving for so long, and no matter what family member of mines, try to console me I just blocked it out. I tried to remember just the good times that my husband and I share for 45 years, but I just keep going back to the night of my tragic moments. It was the most horrible night of my life, I seen my life flash right before me.

Nor my husband or I were strong enough, to fight off this intruder, the fact remains, maybe he just did want the money, but at that time all I could think was we came to the end of our road. You know Erma, you don't know what is on someone mind, at the time they are committing these crime, and I tried telling the young man, we didn't have any money, but he insisted on not leaving empty handed. My husband Marshal, as always was there to protect me from any hurt, harm and danger. Sometimes I think deep down inside, that our attacker, was not there to do any harm, I believe that he was more afraid then we were.

I also feel for him, he could have been a family member of mine, and out there attacking someone else. No matter what Erma, life is what you make it. I really would like to see this guy, and see what he has to say, the lost of my husband bother me a lot, but the person who committed this crime, has to have thoughts soon or later about what they did. If I were a little younger, and even much stronger, I would go and see this fellow, just to have conversation, this way I will understand from both sides of the story.

No Erma it is not right what another human being bring upon others, in such derange ways, but I do think about, will just serving time help these peoples. There should be some other system beside jail time or life in prison. If it was a drug related problem, then why not seek professional help alone with serving time. I mean will these people rehabilitate, it doesn't justify the crime. But they never got the chance to tell their story.

It has to be a reason why. And since that night I have not shaken off this thought as I speak. How do you feel Erma, what do you think, that serving time in jail, is really going to solve problems, I don't know, maybe it just the kind good heart that I have for other people. Or maybe some of them like to be institutionalized.

Whatever the exact nature is, we all have skeletons in our closet. I know it is beyond my beliefs.

You know what Mrs. Pierce, it is so true, and you cannot judge a book by its cover. I have a niece, who was attending her last year in college, to become a Lawyer in 1997.

Her parents were in a plane crash in 1996. Belinda being the only child everything was left to her. Belinda didn't have many cousins on her father side of the family; it was just my brother and I. Her mom was from Georgia, and that is where her family remains.

So she became acquainted, with a few of the student on campus. Then one day a male friend needed somewhere to stay. Belinda felt she knew Darren well enough to trust him, so she rented out the quest-house. It didn't take long for Darren to become comfortable, he really liked Belinda, but she often told him that she was not interested.

So six months went by and Darren comes home, only this time he was intoxicated. Darren then goes over to see Belinda. Not knowing that she had company, this really upset Darren as he watched though the patio door.

After Belinda Company leaves her home, Darren rings her door bell. When she goes to answer, he became distraught and angry, pushes Belinda inside put a gun to her head and rapes her. My niece is now in a mental institution, she hasn't been herself for a long time. Belinda went into a state of shock that night.

You know Erma let's talk about something else; this is really getting me pretty upset, although it did help me to talk about my circumstances. As a matter of fact, let get up off these chair, get on our knees, and pray to the Good Lord, for the great things in life, that we have seen and were able to enjoy. Also we will pray for the lost soul in this world, that peace and hope comes upon them to find their way, and this can be a better place to live.

As long as we have some time on our side, it is never too late, to change your life around and walk in the right path. So let's burn a couple of candles, turn off the lights, and get real busy, I am sure there are a lot of other peoples out there, that is doing the same thing we are about to do right now. I believe prayer is power.

Chapter Three

THE SECURITY OFFICER

During the time, that this tragic incident was being occurred, an Officer by the name of Harvey Whitehead who worked for this community took the call. Being that Harvey was the only Security Officer on the premises at the time; he called for a security team, and then dialed 911.

Harvey who is in his late forty has been with Protocol Security Company, for 15 years, and has never received a phone call this dramatic in all his life. He has dealt with several other situations, in this community, such as fights breaking out, loud music being played at a very late time. Many cars have been stolen from the parking lot. Even the young crowd, hanging under tenants window cursing and carrying on.

A few minutes later, when his back up arrived, Harvey and his partner Kirk Able pursuit to walk over to the complex, in which the call was made. As he entered the complex, Whitehead could hear the noises coming from the apartment above. Kirk you stay down here, just in case there's another way out. He walked upstairs approached the door to the Pierce's apartment. While he stood facing the apartment door, the door then opened and the defendant walked out.

Whitehead not knowing what to do or say thought that this person might have live here. He then asked what was going on; the defendant "answered" "There's nothing going on just came by to see how family was doing. Whitehead then responded to the defendant, I just got a call, stating there was a robbery in progress. Robbery, why would anyone think that, this was not such a bad area to live in. Whitehead then asked the defendant to wait, as he checks out things.

However 15 seconds later while Whitehead was speaking on his radio, the defendant suddenly bolted down the stairs.

He rushed out of the complex, so fast; he nearly knocked over Able, who was standing on watch. Able at the time was looking up at the fire escape to be aware of anyone coming out. Able was not prepared in apprehending the defendant, in which he gotten away. Whitehead then ran down the stairs after the defendant, by this time the defendant ran through the complex, for quite some time, before he was apprehended by, another Security Officer named Webster Calloway. At this point, Security Officer Tara Brother and her partner Guy Nelson had also responded to the scene.

Defendant was then handcuff, and placed in the Security Vehicle with Officer Brother. Whitehead returns to the apartment complex, in which the incident occurred. As Whitehead approached the door, it opened and he was shocked to see the victims, Mrs. Pierce appearance, her numerous bruises, and swollen arm.

Whitehead then radioed for an EMS unit for both Mrs. Pierce and Her husband Marshall, who was hurt up better badly, moving very sluggishly, and barely able to speak, because of their age and how upset they become during the attack. Just stay calm Whitehead replied, help is on the way. As they waited for EMS to arrive Whitehead, started questioning Mrs. Pierce, about what has happen this night. Mrs. Pearce all shaken up was just too concerned about her husband welfare.

So here we have it, a typical Security Officer, just doing his job for his community, when suddenly, out of nowhere an assault and robbery takes place. Right up under his nose. At this time where was his partner, why was Whitehead working alone in a 200-300 unit complex thank GOD he knew how to respond to such a situation, that it did not cause him his life. The suspect was apprehended and Whitehead was acknowledging for his bravery.

Chapter Four

THE HOSPITAL

Upon the arrival at Green Memorial Hospital in the City of Cincinnati, when the Pierce were brought into the emergency room, awaiting to be examine by the trauma surgeon Dr. Vincent Aponte. Because of the attack Mr. Pierce received, Dr. Aponte ordered a CAT scan of his head to rule out internal head injuries. Mr. Pierce was already a sick elderly man, who was diagnosed that he had been on blood thinner called Coumadin. When the CAT scan result were, returned Dr. Aponte, notice some collection of blood around Mr. Pierce brain.

Later on after taking an x-ray, Dr. Aponte then notified a Neurosurgeon and surgical team to help him handle his case. During this time Mrs. Pierce was begin examined, just a little shaking up at the time, a pretty bruised face and swollen arm, which was put in a arm sling, a sedative was given to help calm her down, all she kept asking was how is my husband. Dr. Aponte insisted that Mrs. Pierce relax so that sedative would help her to sleep, and that her husband would be all right. Mrs. Pierce was release the next morning. Several other CAT scan had been taking though out the next day, and found that Mr. Pierce condition was stable and that there was no significant pressure on his brain.

After this procedure the surgeon placed him in the Intensive Care Unit for observation.

Now during Mr. Pierce stay in this hospital, the doctors decided that they would experience on this patient. Mr. Pierce was issued 3 units of fresh frozen blood plasma this was to help reverse the blood level of the Coumadin. Considering the amount of blood plasma, Mr. Pierce would also be administering medications for high blood pressure. Still being monitor after having the plasma no effect had occurred at this time.

Although the Pierce's were both able and very conscious at the time of their arrival, they were also talkative and very well alerted. Once Mrs. Pierce was released, she had to be questioned by the arresting police officers. She was taken down to the station from the hospital to identify the suspect. During her leave Dr. Vincent Aponte informed her that her husband would be well cared for. She would have nothing to worry about. He is in the best of hands.

During this time still being monitor, Mr. Pierce condition had remain the same. Minutes, hours, and 2 days have gone by still no changes in the patient condition. After overlooking the patient for any bruises or lacerations marks, Dr. Aponte notice swelling behind the left side of the ear. This was a horrible tragedy that took place to this elderly couple. Dr. Aponte also noticed that the patient didn't have any fracture to his skull nor his head. He did consider that maybe some of Mr. Pierce injuries was consistent either being beaten or kicked quite a few times with someone hands or by his foot.

There are all types of tragedy each and every day. People young and old are in and out the emergency rooms. Some don't even make it to the Operating table. Just innocent victims being attacked by such violent acts of immorality, it is very disturbing. Not knowing when, where, or how, at any given time, some hardly had the chance to even identify their attackers. As they said this is a free country, wherever did they get that idea from? There will always be a price to pay, no matter what the circumstances are nothing is free.

So during the time of Mr. Pierce observation, family members, and friends all gather together, in the waiting area patiently, waiting on his results. Sorry to say that he expired on the tenth day. This really brought about trauma within this family. How do you react to such violent, and mishaps. When it is so close to home, anger, frustration, hatred, hurt all at once. Do we even get the chance to think, before we are ready to respond to such situations, that we are really powerless over anyhow.

Where will it lead us to, greater pain for a bigger price to pay? From my experience I came very close to a situation as this one, I tell you about that another time. It is hard and no one ever said life would be easy, but most of it depends on us. It is what we make of it; either complicated or keeps it simple, and without GOD in our lives, or lives is meaningless as well as complicated. So my prayers go throughout the whole world, don't just read because it is a book, read with any open-mind and an open heart, that our prayers be heard and answered.

Chapter Five

THE JURY

Victoria Worth

One day Victoria Worth and her two twin girls Alicia and Felicia, who is 5 years of age, were on their way downtown to see about getting some food stamps. Victoria who is 29 year old African American a single parent and lives in a studio apartment for the last 2 ½ years. Recently was laid off her job as a cashier at the A & P Supermarket, for coming up short on the register at least 3 times a week, she lived in the project not far from where her children's went to school.

Victoria had always wanted to go back to school, after giving birth to the girls, but for some reason she believed she was in love, with the girls papa who never gave a second thought or look at Vicky. He used and abuse her so bad that she thought she would never amount to anything in life. She became depress, stressed and out of breath, speechless because she was that much afraid of Jeffery.

As time went on Vicky knew that she wanted to do the right thing for herself and her children's. so she went down to the courthouse to apply for clerical work. She put several application in at City Hall, but what Vicky was applying for required skills. At this time

Jeffery didn't want Vicky to achieve her goals, so he told her that it was him or her career, much as in love Vicky thought she was, it brought tears to her eyes thinking that she couldn't live without Jeffery.

She didn't know what to do at this point, all she knew is that her life had to change for the better, if she stay within this relationship it was bound to get worst, tired of all the aggravation and disrespect she decided to leave Jeffery. It was hard because Jeffery put up a fight for a family that he had no care for. He didn't want anyone else to have his family, and Victoria told him that is not the reason why I am leaving you.

I need to get my life together so that my children's can grow up the right way, knowing whatever it is you want or need it is a struggle. Do not make the same mistake that I have made with my life, I am going back to school to get a degree in Law. Right now I just need you to get out of my face. I am beginning to know now that is wasn't love that I felt for you it was fear of leaving you. An argument broke out and Jeffery decides he would start beating on Victoria the neighbors heard the commotion and this brought about the police.

Vicky was hospitalize for 5 day with a broken arm and busted eye, her sister Monique came and took care of the girls until Vicky was well. A Ms. Conner from the battered home for women came to see Victoria at the hospital just before her release. She offered Vicky to come and stay at the shelter with her children's no one had to know where they were.

That was a good decision that Victoria made because she was able to get a 2 bedroom apartment for low income and a part-time job in sales. She also plan to go back to school as soon as possible to get her degree. Vicky went down to City Hall so much putting in applications, that her name came up for jury duty. What a wonderful opportunity she thought this would be for her.

Victoria had no idea where this case would be leading her into. At the time, she just felt well it is a start, I get to know some of these people down here, at the court house, or maybe I can land a job. Whatever the outcomes are, just think they just may pay for my schooling in law. It just a dream of mine, but dreams sometimes comes true, if you want it bad enough.

So Vicky went about telling Alicia and Felicia about the good news that, she had just received in the mail. Oh I am so excited; I can hardly wait for this date, to know that I was picked for jury

Duty; this must be a great opportunity to put on my resume. Oh girls I can't wait to tell Nana. She thought that I would never leave your dad. I remember telling me self about dreams they have already started coming true.

Victoria called Ms. Conner and told her the news, how wonderful; Ms. Conner replied when you start. Well this is November the 27th a couple of weeks from now; I do have to go down to the Courthouse in a week to give my information, and to get what case I will be assigned too.

Days have gone by, and Vicky had received her assigned case, when she was told of the case, she became very horrified. For Victoria was to be on jury duty for a murder case. Nothing that she ever thought would be her first assignment. Oh what am I to do? Vicky knew she could not discuss the case with anyone. So her best bet was to go to the library and to do some research on the case to get some can of insight of what she was up against.

Vicky had 3 days left for jury duty, and her time clock was ticking faster than ever. All she could do was pace the floor back and forth, wiping her forehead, she finally decided let me get a hold of myself. After all this is what I want to go to school for, to be a lawyer, and a pretty good one at that. I know it will be a struggle for life has many obstacles that we will have to face. Whoever said life would be easy. One thing I know throughout my relationship with Jeffery, life is what you make it if, you not putting nothing into it, you will get nothing out of it.

So there all I had to do was give myself a good pep talk, and you know what it worked, I can conquer anything that is positive, all I need is patience, hope, faith and a lot of prayer and to believe that there is a power greater than myself, I know because for one thing it took me ten years to believe in myself, because of a bad relationship that I did not know how to come out of, my faith is the size of a mustard seed, which has now fertilized. I will put on my seatbelt; this is going to be a devastating ride.

Chante Self

A very thin weighing 110 pounds, 5_5 with big bubbly eyes, sides of a 50 cent piece. African American female name Chante Self. 33 year old high school drop-out and from a family of 12 siblings. Chante is the third from the youngest not a bad looking female, medium complexion, short hair-cut, faded on the sides. Chante is a very self center individual about everything under the sun.

She has the tendency of knowing everything for a high school drop-out. Her parents have been telling Chante for the last 5 years to go back to school. Now or never you are always in and out of our house. You need somewhere stable to lie down your head. Why don't you get the newspaper and do some job searching if you do not know what you want to do at this time with yourself . . .

Constantly talking day in and day out, Chante do you ever think about your son Marquee, do you plan on raising him, or you rather his papa family have all the privileges of raising our grandchild. Oh mom come on get off of the subject just let me think will you, I got the situation under control. I just been thinking over some things and it is taking quite some time to arrange my plans. My girlfriend Olivia she said, there is an opening at the factory where she work, and they pay pretty good. So I do have any interview tomorrow, see I took my first step. If this works out then I will start doing better mom.

Living down here on Mulberry Lane in the projects, it is not so simple that I can go back to school and overnight accomplish my goals, I want out of here; I do plan on doing the right thing for myself and my son. But not here it is too much drama; you could hardly stick your head out of the window, without someone over top of you, dumping their trash. I know I have given you and pop a hard way to go and I apologize for that. I have been stubborn, foolish, and very self-center because I wasted a lot of my time doing nothing, and thinking something would just fall from the sky and happen for me.

By the way you and pop do know I use this address for my mail to come, so when I do my interview tomorrow, they will forward my w-2 forms here. If I could do it all over again I would, as soon as I get on my feet and financially situated, I plan to move to North Carolina, what part that I could not answer yet. I just want to move out of Ohio, with a fresh new start, attitude and outlook. Olivia family is having a family reunion in a month and I have been invited to take the trip to North Carolina with them, I can then look around a little and get an ideal of my new environment.

Well mom the trip to the North was terrific, and I decided to go back in two weeks, I know where me and Marquee will be living, Fayetteville, North Carolina, isn't that just wonderful mother. I come to a time in my life where I finally can take control, no more self pity, or self pride I can now move on to better things in life. Chante I really hate to burst your bubble, but while you were gone on your little trip, I don't think you will be making another one in two weeks, you receive mail during your absent, and I think it something you would really like.

What could it possibly be, I haven't applied for any other job and my schooling I just decided what it is I wanted to do. I decided I am going to school to be a publisher. In what category, well that is another decision. So come on tell me, oh I know my w-2 forms has arrived.

No Chante I don't think so, who in the world could be writing me, oh Olivia cousin Bernard who is so gorgeous, tall and handsome, I met him during the reunion, that who it is right mom. Here Chante stop guessing and take the letter please. Oh my goodness, Oh my goodness, what am I suppose to do with this, I have no experience in jury duty.

Now only that it is in 2 weeks, when I am suppose to be going back to North Carolina, what am I going to do now. I have to find a way of getting out of this one. I know call and tell them that I am still down North, will you mom. Now Chante you know I cannot do that, just go to jury duty it may be the best thing for you. The best things for me how and in what way, please tell me so I know how to handle the matter. If I never listen to you before I am all ears now.

Chante it is not as bad as you are making it to be, just go exchange your information, and see where it will led you from there. You don't have a choice of the matter, there will be a penalty, and you will never make it back down North any time soon. Yeah I guess you are right mom, the choice wasn't mine in the first place, and if I stop doing things my way all time, and do GOD Will, it could only get better. So from this point I will have any open-mind and take any suggestion that will help me throughout the rest of my life. Thank you parents for being so supportive and putting up with me and not giving up on me. For that I am truly grateful.

Kevin Ptashkin

Let me introduce myself, my name is Kevin Ptashkin, I am a 47 year old Hispanic with an associate degree, in computer science. I been married twice and have 5 children's between the two marriages. And believe me child support is dramatically increasing as time goes on. I am now a single man, because neither marriage worked out for me, I was afraid of commitment, as well as the responsibilities of being a family man.

My first marriage was right out of high school, when I was nineteen years of age. And my first baby girl was born by the time I turned 22 years of age. By the time my 23rd birthday rolled around I attended my first year of college. After the first two semesters my second child was born.

He was named after me, we called him K.P. for short, his mom of cause wanted to name him after her dad, and his name was Walter. My son would have never forgiven me if I agreed to his grandpapa name.

As time went on I began putting my career before my family, I even sometimes spend more times with my friends then I did at home. I wanted to get a room on campus to get away from the responsibilities that I had at home; all I would think about was I. What I wanted, when I wanted it. My wife Tina became very frustrated that she had to pull the wagon on her own. She decided that we should separate until the matter was resolved. I agreed to do this and visit bi-weekly to see the children's and Tina.

Later on during my visitation with my family, things started dwelling down, where there was no call no show. I had a little freedom I took advantage of the situation. I started to disrespect my wife and showboat as though I had it going on. She was a very good mother and woman. I felt because I had the freedom, this was the opportunity to get to know someone else. That definitely was grounds for divorce. I had two more years to complete my study and to receive my degree.

Within a year and half I met a woman name Vanessa, we became quite close and intimate, I knew there was no turning back now. I tried to fill the void that I had within me from the lost of my first family. I thought this time I make it work, in a half of year Vanessa was pregnant with my twin sons. I then propose to marry her the following year after my graduation. I landed a good job in Computer Science bringing at the table about $80 grand a year.

I knew then I had it made. What a surprise I had when my second wife was pregnant with our third child, our daughter Gevalia was born the youngest of the five children's the seeds that I planted, I now placed more value on myself than ever before. I realized that I fear the fact of being a papa and a husband.

My oldest child was now 25 years of age, and my youngest was 10 years old. They knew about the other sibling, but I did not have the time for them to get to know one another. I stayed with Vanessa just until she had enough of my childish behavior, I let my job go to my head and I forgot where I came from. I never gave myself the chance to know who I was, I ran from all responsibilities if I felt I was under any pressure. It took me two marriages to come to a complete understanding that I was afraid to face my fears. I now have two families out there in the world that I was not providing well for at all, I wanted everything for myself. How selfish of me, to take anyone for granted, what gives me the right to underestimate anyone.

My parents they only wanted the best for their children's, I guess they over did it when it came to me, because I didn't know how to share anything, just knew how to take. So I eventually had to move of the house of my second family, their mothers were good with them, how they explain the drama that I caused in their lives were unspeakable they barely would talk about it.

As time went on my ex-first wife Tina, have gotten information pertaining to my second ex-wife Vanessa. She called Vanessa and they arranged to meet at Tiffany on Lane Drive the following day. They wanted to become friends and for the children's to get to know one another, something that I didn't have in mind, could not care less. That was my way of thinking selfish, very selfish.

I was happy to see the family come together after awhile, Vanessa would call every now and then on my cell phone. The last time she called me she told me she had some very important mail for me. I told her now was not the time, and could I pick it up in a week or two, Vanessa said I think you better come as soon as possible.

So I agreed to come over to the house to pick up my mail, only to be surprise of what was to be expected. There were two letters one, stated jury duty, and the other well figure it out for youself, yes divorce papers. It seem like my whole world had close in on me, as though it was the end of the world for me, I had no one to turn to here I made all this money lost both family and wasn't happy at all. And a thought passed through my mind something is missing, the greatest inspiration of all GOD, I now know without him my life was meaningless. The Associate Degree, the money nothing meant anything more to me at that time, I now had to face reality on a daily basis, and being on jury duty was a challenge.

Dominic Halfpenny

Well the time finally came, it is my turn to serve Jury Duty, how utterly convincing. Just a month and half ago my wife Jeanette, and I was sitting at the breakfast table having, grits, eggs, muffins, and a glass of OJ. Along with a cup of fine roasted coffee, with the aroma of hazelnut creamer. I was then reading an article in the Saturday Media newspaper, when I happen to come across the jury duty list for the upcoming cases. It took me by surprise to expect myself as a juror.

It's funny I watch the news daily, I read the newspaper quite often, and if I not doing either then there the radio playing. Broadcasting news all over the place. At one time back in the day when it was quite comfortable, and a very pleasant atmosphere here in Ohio, my community was well respected, it was like everyone was everyone's neighborhood watcher. As time went on without any thought the world changed. I am 43 year old Caucasian guy, from a family of four children's, three sisters, and I am next to the oldest.

My parents who were from Tennessee, decided to move us from the country part to the city. I found that most interesting, because my mom was kind of set in her own way, really homey like. I was 13 years of age when we moved to Ohio, it took me time to adjust to my new environment; my style was that of a nerd, I had no idea how to dress, as well as how to impress. I have always wanted to go to school for Journaling, but my family just could not afford to send all their children's.

Then during the summer when I was old even to start my summer job, I deliver newspapers. I believe that is why I am so much of a news buff now. There was nothing I could not tell you that I read in the paper. Mr. Nickel one of my customers always would ask me to tell him what the stocks look like today. Mrs. Eagle had a house full of children's she would order then news paper but never have time to read it. Her favor section was classified; she just couldn't wait for those children's to be old even for her to start working. She wanted to know different opportunities that were out there between now and then.

I deliver newspapers for the next five years, and I then signed myself up to a Community College for a Journalist Course. Completed my course in four years, and did my intern at Media News, which I am now their lead Journalist. It took time and effort to accomplish my goal, I did succeed, and this is where I met my wife, happily married for 12 years. You think about the different challenges that life has, and some of the things that you think about doing most thing don't even get done. Well somebody has to do it, and now that I have the opportunity to be on a juror, I am so over excited about the case, I just cannot wait to meet the different peoples in which I have to deal with all personalities what a challenge for my new article.

Valencia Brookdale

Simple minded but a much created outgoing female with an African American father, and a Caucasian mother. I have one brother and one sister and I am the youngest, I also have a daughter 3 years of age, her name is Serenity. I am 27 years old and have my own place on the West Side from my parent's location. I am proud to say that my parent's marriage was a success, after 35 years, the flame still burns. My father works for the city of Ohio now for 28 years, and my mom she works for Cake and Bake Catering for 13 years of course she had to raise her family before she could ever leave the house.

Me I am unwed and still dating my daughter father 6 ½ years, Brian is trying to establish a career in Automobiles Detailing to own his business and build a future for us, while I am maintaining my career in Interior Decorating. I love to sew, cook, as well as reading, I read every night to Serenity before her bed time. Maybe later on in the future, both Brian and I talk about having more children's. I am much overprotected about my daughter, whenever she leaves my sight it so devastating to find many children's abuse as well as missing from their homes. It a horrible thing to think about knowing and not knowing what circumstances can come your way.

I been living at my address well over 2 years, it quite a pleasant neighborhood, crime is everywhere, the more you pay to live better, the worst some things become, I just pray day and night for peace and happiness. I go to school at night while Brian works during the day, so far our situation is not complicated at all, and I guess we both know what we want. One good aspect that came out of me going to school at night is that it doesn't interfere with my going to jury duty. I was not happy at all when I received this notice, I practically lost it for about 45 minutes, hovering and hollering all over the place, my daughter was kind of frighten. I finally calmed down after hearing her ask me over and over mommy what jury duty? Trying to explain to a 3 year old was like not ever wanting her to find out what sex was all about. Here I am thinking where to begin, wondering if I tell her will this have an effect on her life.

Jury Duty what a headache I had, just saying the word, I could not wait to Brian got home maybe he could explain better than me, so I try to change the subject, Serenity just keep repeating the question, I told her when dad comes home we will talk about, I knew by then she would fall asleep.

But this particular evening, which was Friday night she knew I did not have school, so she decided to wait for her dad to come home. Ok I said Serenity Jury Duty is something a lot of people do not like to do. For instance me, it is when you are subpoena to come to court, what is subpoena mommy? And what is court? Look Serenity let just lay down and close our eyes take a small nap until dad gets home. We will talk about later when dad gets home, now I see where she got repeating the same thing over and over again from, look how bout you wait to mother goes to Jury Duty in 3 weeks and I will tell you all about it.

Chance Washington

Born and raised in the City of Philadelphia, amongst 8 siblings, I am next to the oldest of five males and three females, my family did not have much, but my dad was in the Army for 35 years, and that is how I ended up here in Ohio. My mom was the ordinary housewife, who dealt with everyone of our personality on a different level of communication. She would always tell me when I was ten years old; she would be very surprised and pleased if someone ever married me in life.

I could not understand my characteristics at this time, and I never would believe anything bad could happen to me. I was selfish, self centered, and spoil, as time went on at the age of 25 years old, I went to college to take a course that I never completed. My older brother Hassan who was the father image whenever dad was away on leave, would always tell me about the way I would handle a situation, I care about no one but myself. I really don't know if this affect was me missing dad, and I just wanted attention. However it caused me a great deal of pain, throughout my life.

All the lessons, experiences that mom and my siblings would warn and tell me about, it was like I was stuck on stupid, I took nothing serious I did not and would not accept my own responsibilities in any way. I was always good at pointing the finger at someone else, if I was not doing that then I would find fault in someone. It became very distraught to those who loved me, I did not have many friends, nor did I stay in a relationship for a long period of time. I was too arrogant and I did not want to hear anything if it had to do with me.

I wouldn't and will not believe that I could be wrong about anything. My way or the highway, I had no idea of knowing how to keep things simple, I would turn the simplest situation into an outrage of confusing. Not knowing when to end the conversation, repeating words from words over and over again. I had a ruin spirit; I feared being wrong and not knowing how to face life on life term, it all balled down to reality. It was time for me to take a personal inventory of myself.

Here I am a full grown African American guy, in and out of relationship like there was no tomorrow, the fact that I was very argumentative human being with no self-control what so ever, whatever came out my mouth whether pleasing or not I never came to find out who I really was. I finally met the sweetest, kindest woman I could ever image.

Deanne was very understanding, and supportive of me, even when I transformed on her, she has been though what I am going though only she knew how to let go. She would always tell me time is short, life is short, and she doesn't take any shorts. She asked me one day what was missing in my life or from my life. That made me so bitter, when only someone tries to help me identify with my pain. I could not even answer her without an argument pursuing. She finally got fed up with my childish behavior, I only want to love you, but it is very hard to love someone who doesn't love themselves.

Everything has to be explain to you, even those things that are self explanatory, it ridiculous Chance, you think you know but yet you lack self education. What is that suppose to mean Deanne? I tell you this much Chance, you have Jury Duty in a couple of weeks, you have bet to get it together, mentally, physically, and spiritually, by prayer and a power that is much higher than you can ever image. You are going to find yourself by yourself, and if for any reason you think you will make it, being alone you better just think again. Because if you cannot deal with logical evaluation on a personal scale, you haven't use the tools given to you. LORD only knows what the outcome is going to be the day you and the others juror make a decision base on another human life. Picture this someone else life in your hands, this will be the longest trial ever known in history.

Henrietta Morristown

I am a 52 year old Caucasian woman, who had struggle most of my life. I was born and raised in Ohio, with both parents, and one sister older than myself. Bernadette is now 56 years old, married and have five children's. I was 48 years of age when my mother deceased, my father Billy Bob is resided in a Nursing Home about 10 miles from my home. Bernadette and I were not close at all, I am a single woman, with no children's, and I figure we didn't have anything in common.

For a long time I had to get to know myself, I could not understand why there was so much confusing going on in our household as children's. Father would come home from work and start to argue with mother constantly bickering all the time, we all knew he was head of household, and he was to be acknowledge all the time. Both my parents were alcoholics. Mother would sneak and do her drinking whenever Bernie or I was off to school. Father he would come home drunk it was like he went to work drinking came back home the same way. I could never understand how he manages keeping his job.

However this went on for years, when I turned 16 years old I had my first boyfriend which my parents have not approved me to date. So I started sneaking around doing want I wanted to do, Bernie at the time had already left home, I did not have anyone much to talk too, both my parents were from very small families, and so they too were not close. I did drop out of school when I turned 17 years old, I thought that I was so much in love; I wanted to follow Johnny around all the time and he too drop out of school. Johnny was 2 years older than me and living a very fast life.

He would take me to the Club Company 2, over in the bricks on Mulberry Lane, where he and his boys Mike, Otis and Billy would party all the time. I thought what a great ideal for him to invite me over to the club, not knowing what was behind closed doors. They had everything going on, things that I never imagine in my life. The music was loud, the lights were psychedelic, the temperature outside was just right, nice summer night to be partying. But then it happens, I was offered my first drink, after that it was the marijuana; wow I thought this is cool.

I had the munchies I couldn't stop laughing, and the drinks kept on coming, I did not know where this road was leading me to, I just knew I loved Johnny and there was nothing I would not do for him. His friend Mike had rolled another joint, by this time I knew what the short term was, drinking and smoking on and on and on, wow I kept saying. All of a sudden I got off the sofa to dance with Johnny and my head started to spin, I was looking down thinking that the floor was moving really fast. By this time I grabbed Johnny and told him that I wasn't feeling too well so he carried me to the bedroom and laid me down, please Johnny I said don't leave me, I be right back he said.

He then left a minute or two by this time I was really didn't know if I wanted to lie down or sit up. He returned in the room and started unbuttoning my blouse, saying take off some of your close, so that you will feel better. I have never undress before in front of Johnny since we started dating did not know what he was up to at this time, I begin pushing him away saying stop everything is moving so fast, just let me alone, I will get it together. Johnny insists that I do as he said and let him help me to undress. Okay Johnny if it will make you feel any better, I just want to sleep this mess off. So he kindly took off my blouse, slowly his hands went down my navel and he began unsnapping my jeans. Lift your body a little he says so I can get your pants off, this way you will sleep better and not be so hot. Okay Johnny as long as you let me be.

Then he said to me let me get you another beer so that it can mellow you down Rita, I always thought whatever Johnny said was okay. I realize only a few minute had gone by, where was Johnny, Otis had come into the room to see if I was alright I just kept asking for Johnny, he said Johnny went to the store and ask him to keep an eye on me. Otis then start rubbing on my back in a very uncomfortable way, I was so drunk it felt okay just for a minute, he then ask me to stretch my arms toward the headboard, I am going to massage your arms, Otis said, instead he hand-cuff my wrist and duct taped my mouth.

He then called Mike and Billy into the room as one held my ankles down they began having all kind of sexual activities with my body. It was the most horrible time of my life, I felt useless, and so humiliated, I did not think what was happening to me would ever come to an end, they constantly continue taking turns with me, Mike then said come on Johnny said not to overdo it, I could not believe what I was hearing, it was so devastating all this time Johnny was part of this horrible ordeal. I felt so sick Otis remove the tape from my mouth, I vomit right in the bed hand-cuffed and all. He told me if I ever told anyone what had happen I would live to see my 18th birthday. I was so afraid I just laid there, in my own mess too weak to move.

As time went on I never seen or heard from Johnny again, nor did I ever forget the horrible ordeal that I was put through, and still today I have never told anyone what happen. Now at the most mature level of my life, I am summoned to serve on Jury Duty, the opportunity to listen to total strangers, and hear both side of their stories, the victim, and the defendant, in knowing whatever the consequences maybe, I hope I make the right choices, because now I have a second chance in overcoming my fears as well as facing them, listening to someone else ordeal similar to mine or even worst.

Warren Causey

Let me introduce myself, my name is Warren Causey, I lived in Norfolk, VA until the age of 23. I attend a Community College at the age of 25 here in Ohio, I always told myself I would not accomplish my goal whatever it would be and still be living in my hometown. Just one of those fellows who had to get away, build and have my own business and later on a wife and children. Well that never came to pass, I was young immature and thought I had all the time in the world to finish completing what I started.

Well it is not easy dreaming and the dream does not come true, it take a lot of honesty and hard work, motivation and beliefs to reach your goals. It all started like this, once I moved to Ohio my major was business. Okay I got into the college because I had some very good grades and I just wanted to stay in school just a little while longer. After majoring the business course I said I would like to open my own Janitorial Service. It took a lot of hard work and studying to get to this level, things started looking up for me and I knew like all the important people, such as Mr. Lindbergh in charge of the on job training programs. He gave me my first assignment at Wal-Mart; my hours were 7:00 p.m. until 10:00 p.m.

There I had to mix certain solution and learn the how to use the buffing machine, it took some time for me to catch on with the machine, at first it was too fast for me and then it was too slow. I finally got it together, I believe it just was my nerves, this was like the happiest moment of my life, I called my mom on my cell phone to tell her about my new position, she was so proud that I was holding my own. Mother raises me and three other brothers, without our father. It was such hard times and I am next to the youngest, Todd gave mom so much trouble, if he was not going to school then he would be somewhere stealing. My oldest brother Tyrone he had ways just like my dad, did not care about anything or anyone.

My middle brother Marcus went off to serve for his country, that worried mom half to death, there comes a time when everyone has to live their life, whether they want something positive for themselves or just live to die, it is not a good thing to say, but this is so true, I watched Todd screw up his life, me and mom both was there for him, Todd was a spoil brat, his way or no way. Things really started getting out of hand, my baby brother Todd, became a substance abuser. It was not a shock to me, and I mom gave him just about anything he wanted, as well letting him get away with murder, she felt she owed Todd something, because dad left us alone at such a young age.

My oldest brother never returned home, Marcus made a life for himself and family, so there was just me and mom trying to keep Todd on the right track. I did have to take a leave of absent during our trials and tribulations, I thought just for a little while. Time went and on and on, things got out of control.

Mother could no longer deal with the headache and heartache that Todd was taking her through. I never knew mother had made any decision without my knowing. I guess this time, no one knew not even Todd.

So one particular day, during the month of June 2003, mom went out looking for Todd. She was in placing she should have never gone. Still no Todd, she then ran into one of the boys from the neighbor, in which she told Kevin, if you see Todd, please tell him to come home right away, there is something I have for him. Finally hours and days have gone by, still no one heard from Todd.

Mother paced the floor just about every night, she would not talk to me about anything, and she just wanted Todd at home. I could not handle this situation any longer, so I told mother she was on her on. I packed my bags and left, the house without any knowledge of where I was going. So I then checked in a cheap Hotel downtown on Raymond Blvd. Just to be close to home for awhile, once I got the key to my room, I took off my shoes, shirt, I then reached for the remote to turn on the television.

What happen next really took me by surprise; the reporters were talking about a double murder, right in my area. So I decided to call mother, when I did not get a answer, I called Ms. Braun our next door neighbor, after hearing that my mother killed my brother Todd, and then took her own life, this left me very wordless. There was nothing else I could do here; I wanted to leave Norfolk, VA after their burial. There was one thing holding me back, from leaving I have been subpoena to court for Jury Duty. The trial was based on a murder case, in which I had no subjection to being there, I was a nervous wreck at the time, and I did not know whether they would excuse me or not for jury duty, I felt like a criminal that jump bail. I finally gave it some thought, and realize a good night sleep is all I need, when the morning come, by then I might have changed my mind. Whatever the case may be, whether I serve jury duty or not, I am out of the State of Virginia for good. Relocate and start a new beginning for myself, and leave the pass behind.

Emilo Lopez

How can I begin, to say I live a very rough life, I was raised by my grandmother, on my father side of the family, in which I never did know my parents. Both my mother and father were drug addicts, who had six children's, in which they did not raise. I was the fourth from the youngest. I had three older sisters, and a younger sister and brother under me. We were born and raised in Porto Rico, so by the time, my fifteen birthdays arrived, grandmother decide to move to Ohio. She would always talk to us about leaving Porto Rico, she just could not bear the pain that my father and mother have caused the family. My oldest sister Camille and my sister Rita would help grandmother around the house, and I would chip in when necessarily, like sweep the floor, take out the garbage, and run small errand for grandmother.

All the children's and myself, would address grandmother with the name Labelle, she wore this small gold chain with a bell attached to it, that she would always use when dinner was being serve, she also would use it whenever we were too far from the house. Grandmother was the kindest caring person anyone would love to have in their family. She took well care of us all, every night at the dinner table, she would tell us a little more about our parents. She tried to make us understand that they loved us, both their lives were headed down the wrong road, but that was no fault of ours. Labelle did the best she could, and we loved her for being honest with the six of us.

At the age of 17 when I graduate from high school, I received my first job, from work study, it was a permanent position, studying criminal justice, working with children, that has been abandon, neglected, or abused. I enjoyed my job very much, I felt after what me and my siblings had to go through, there was always someone, doing just as bad. I was then transfer to the courthouse, to do my internship, this was the most interesting job, I could ever want. I study so many cases than ever, by the time I was twenty-one, I was working for the courthouse. I wanted to change my position, and possibly become a Parole Officer for the state. I know whatever I wanted to do; it had to be within the system of society. I had some doubt along the way, because of my nationality. Most of the time, I would feel very intimidated, it took some time but I finally realized, that life was not fair. I believed in myself, and I became good at whatever it was that I did.

My sisters and brother, all became talented in their careers, Labelle was so proud of raising her grandchildren's so well, it did not bother her, that my father made those choices in his life, he had the knowledge and wisdom to know right from wrong, he choice to live without morality and conduct himself in a good manner. Grandmother raised my father alone grandfather, died when dad was three years old, and he was the only child, he did not have a bad life, as I can speak for myself, the proof is with the six of us, and grandmother is much older now. She always did what was right by my dad. He was just one of those kinds of people who took everything and everyone for granted. So the time has come, everyone in the family became successful, Labelle was too proud of us all she would cry every time she looked our way. So the entire sibling decided that Labelle deserve a vacation, we were all old enough to look after one another. We sent grandmother on a two week cruise to Hawaii, she was every so happy, being she never did anything for herself in such a long time.

By this time my older sister was thirty-two, and I was twenty-five years of age, so there was no need for grandmother to worry, she knew that we were very dependable adults, and she did a good job raising us. So my career starting advancing more and more, I really enjoyed the criminal system, in helping others get their lives back on the right track, it was something to really think about, having another human life in your hand, as though you can control them by the snap of your fingers. Finally I advance my position in becoming a Parole Officer for the state. I was very pleased with this position; it put me in a better position to help people, especially the young ones.

I would arrive at work by 7:30 a.m. and sometimes I would be there until 9:00 p.m. at night and then every other Saturday until 7: p.m., I took my job very seriously; I really wanted to help those who needed. Every now and then I would always imagine myself climbing the ladder of success, just my imagination of one day being a judge, I know it would take a lot time and hard work, I was not that prepare at the time, my mind and body were not on the same page. At times I like to think what it would be like to be on jury duty, to experience the victim and defendant pain.

Well what a coincide, just so happen on Friday night went I returned home, I got comfortable and poured my a small glass of Chablis Champagne, picked up my mail and kicked back in the recliner chair. By surprise a summon to appear for jury duty in one week, there is a season and a reason. Of course I had to share this with my sibling and the day of jury duty, why that is when grandmother arrive back home. I am so excited this gives me the opportunity to meet more peoples of all walks of life. What a challenge . . . .

Kennedy Marksman

Fifty-six year old veteran, who will soon be retiring in another 5 years, I was married three times and all marriages failed. I know now why my marriages did not last, I was an alcoholic and I did not hold many jobs. As time went on I became more and more depend on alcohol, I had to do something better and turn my life around. I was losing everything I had. I became thin, weak and so fragile if I fell, I probley would have broken every bone in my body.

I was born and raised in Ohio, I joined the Marines as soon as I came out of high school, I did five years of the Marines, and five years in the Navy, there is where I met my wives. Out of the three marriages I had four children's who was so ashamed of me it was to embarrass to stick and stay so, there is where the divorces came in. I believe and sometimes I try and think what started me to drinking. I enjoyed serving the military, but every now and then I would want to be with my family.

My parents was killed in a plane crashed, when I was eleven years of age, going on a trip to Florida, I was the only sibling and my grandparents they did not want to have anything to do with me at all. I could never understand why, there was just too many secrets in our family. My dad parents were deceased, and I used to hear grandmother always telling dad, that mom parents were the strangest people she could ever know. I never visit mom parents that often anyway I guessed it had something to do with who she married. But as time went on I would say to myself when I am old enough to be on my own I will begin my family, and dependable and dedicated as a family man.

Well that did not happen, I believed that I was tormented as a child in one case or another by my mom parents. I do remember being taken to the emergency room a few times, when I was four and six years of age. I was molested as a child by my grand-parents and I buried this beneath all the pain that I suffered. It was just hard to believe that family members can do such things to children's.

I just wanted to get away from it all and start over, so my choice was to join the service and become a man and handle my business. Instead I just ran away from my past not handling the different issue that kept haunting me throughout my life. I started drinking at the age of twenty-two, but I had things under control, it just was a matter of time before I lost control.

So serving time as a Marine, I just love putting on that uniform, and the gloves I felt so whole, and that I was doing the right thing, I never knew looking back on my life now, what the outcomes would be. All I know is that I was on the right track and my life was going to be the best that I could make it. So time went on and I finished the Marines in 1995. I waited a year later and joined the Navy, I met my third wife in Germany had a daughter by her, and three years before I finished the Navy we were divorced. My drinking increased and things started getting out of control.

I decided to move back to Ohio and admit myself into a detoxify center for counseling and some help, I just could not live this life any more, I was washed up and washed out. I lost my family and just about everything I had ever worked so hard for, I looked at myself in the mirror and did not know who it was I was looking at. So I fell to my knees and I prayed with all the breath in my body, for guidance, direction and the right thing to do. I made the phone call to the hospital in which I was being accepted, got the plane tickets, and I was out of there. I returned to Ohio and I did eighteen months in a rehabilitation center. I began to like myself again and I remain confident within myself.

I got me a job working in TGI Friday's as a cook, that is what I specialized in the Navy, I did part-time work on the weekend, as a PC Technician, this is the course I had in the Marine. I know now as being a child that the things that happen to me was not my fault, I had to face my fears so, that I could move on to another level in life. I got a two bedroom apartment, and I started looking though the phone books to locate my children's. I needed to tell them how sorry I was and the pain I caused their mothers, and myself. I can now be whatever I want with hope and faith, which I do not have to look back into my pass as a negative. I am in Ohio now three years and never would think I would serve as a juror on jury duty. The time has come for me to stand for something and to be someone or fall for anything, and I did that very well. I will go serve again for what I stand for, and be the best that I can be, time is of essence.

John Royster Jr.

An unforgettable moment in life, when a time comes for everyone to know their limits. Well I am about to tell you a story about my life history. I was born and raised in Gastonia, North Carolina, with only one brother and no sisters, my papa and mother was never married. We were struggling from the very beginning of our lives. Both parents were from dysfunctional families, in which they did not have the right tools to instill in us. They knew only what they were told and brought only what they were sold. Me and my brother Harold which was one year younger than I, at this time I was nine. My papa John SR. had a job outside of Charlotte N.C. where he did construction work, he did not allow mama to do any outside work, and she was strictly a housewife. They were not much that dad would allow mama to do, she did not have many friends, she hardly went out, always taking care of him, me and my brother and the housework.

Sometimes I would ask mama, dad was too hard on her, she once told me the story of their relationship, that my papa was a womanizer. I asked her how come she puts up with his error, all she can say was, she loved him. I always wonder how can someone love someone else so much more than himself or herself. She sometime still does not trust him to today, that is why they was never married, and had many children's. My papa also had a temper he wanted things done when he spoke about the matter. He sometimes would wake my brother and me up in the wee of the morning to chop wood, or anything just to make mama feel unease. I can say as I got older I was seeing my papa for what he really was, a drunk, womanizer and physically and a verbal abusive person. He sometimes would come into our room at night as though he was making up for his mistakes, and would just repeat the same act over and over again. Mama did not know how to handle the matter; she just became a nervous wreck. So as time went on and I became older I started to stand up to my papa.

My brother Harold was sixteen and I was seventeen, Harold would say are you sure you would like to go up against dad, I had no choice our lives were at stake, and mama begin drinking. Mama has been so confined to the house she started taking papa side even when he would hit her. I sometime wonder what is inside of people heads to behave in such a manner. Does it start from your childhood, or from abusive relationships? Whatever the circumstances are it does not make it right.

Dean Jones

I am a five foot nine inches tall, very petite, thirty-five years of age, working at the United State Postal Service. Well I have been on this job, since I left college, this was not what I had in mind, but I did work my way up to supervisor and I have twenty-five years in the business. I am a single black female, with no children. I am my parents only child, and happy to say, there are still married. Me I'm just an old fashion work alcoholic, my mom is always asking when will I have time for a man, I told her I just do not have any time for the foolishness.

Well De'Ann mother said, what you are doing to yourself, and becoming is very foolish, you are thirty-five years of age with no children, no husband, no apartment, me and your dad will be just fine, please by all means get a life, who knows me and dad may out live you. Are you happy with your job; is this what you would like to do for the next twenty years? I guess you are right mother; I need to mingle, get out more often, and find some friends that I am compatible with. I see the same people on the job every day; I just could not see myself partying with them too.

Do not forget I am the supervisor, not saying I am better, but supervisors hang with supervisors and the ones on my job they're all males, and I do not want to be seen with them, that would really upset the women. I would be getting all the attention. You know mom it's this guy name Alan who work at the Courthouse right across the street from the Post Office, every now and then I catch him looking my way, we never gotten the chance to greet. Besides me always wanting to be a model and an actress during my high school years, I also thought about working for the criminal system, I believe I can make a difference.

I have not dated in so long mother, I would not even know the first thing to say to Alan, beside him asking me out for a date, how will I react when he confront me? Nothing beats a failure but a

Trier, anyway, is there any mail for me today? Yes there is De'Ann, and I think you will be quite amazed once you see what it is. Oh mother if it is not a love letter, what could possibly surprise me? I just go and see for myself. Oh this cannot be, please mother pinch me, I finally will get the opportunity to say something to Alan, and I have been picked for jury duty what a privilege. I am going to use this opportunity to the best of my ability, so that I would familiarize myself with those who have been in the criminal justice for at least ten to twenty years, and maybe just maybe I can change my career.

Well I have few weeks to submit this card back to the courthouse, so I think I will go upstairs, now and just ponder over what it is going to be like, meeting and greeting people of all walks of life, and just what kind of case this will be, I really do not have the time now, for those postal workers, I am going to be working for the courthouse, right after work tomorrow I am going to the library to do some research on criminal cases.

Chapter Six

THE JUDGE

Noel Haverford

Born and raised in Buffalo, New York, with both parents and five sisters, I was the only son and the youngest. My dad whom work in the system as a Captain at a Correctional Facility for twenty-five years in New York, and was transferred to Ohio, to complete his retirement, dad was pleased to be relocated, I was 23 years old at the time, I am now 33 years old and a Judge at the Courthouse in Ohio. I have been on the bench four years and two months. I deal with criminal cases, and I have seen many, many cases in that short period of time.

My family is military inclined, mom was a nurse, dad court marshal, two of my sisters whom are twins were into cardiology, my oldest sister was a lawyer and Sheena my youngest sister served in the service as paramedic. I wanted to become part of society and do something more challenging and I guess you can say I took a risk. Being a Judge is not an easy job to succeed in this world. I have dealt with many criminals and their family some I had compassion for and other just was not deserving of my time. Everyone deserves a second chance in life if they really learn a lesson from the mistakes that they made in life, but who am I to judge.

I am in the Courthouse five days a week; I see people come and go, the same faces, two to five times within a two year sentence. Most of my criminal cases are very much disturbing, but I have a job to fulfill, and I let nothing and nobody get in my way. I take on twenty-twenty five cases a week, twelve hours a day. Yes at times I do think maybe I should have taken up another professional job, computer technician, or skilled carpenter, electrician, my goal when I did four year in the Marines and 6 years of college getting my bachelor and science degree to become a Judge seem so long, but when I look back I am still young and accomplish much in a short period of time.

Some night I actually have nightmares over many of my cases, I wake up in a sweat, as though I am part of the problem, I never discussed these things with my parents or my sisters, but at times I do become afraid. I would like to try and understand a person reason for their error, many of my cases the defendant had to be evaluated by a psychologist, because of their mental behavior, some criminal cases was drug addiction and others were assaults. However I would look over these cases for hours to come to a complete decision. One thing I know for sure is that, being a Judge you cannot let a lot of outside interference bothers you mentally, spiritually, physically or emotionally, because this has and can affect the mind in so many ways, that you may not want to review the case as it should be done, or you can acquire a bad attitude towards these criminals, at times because you see them come and go all day long.

I have to be honest with myself, there were times, and I did favors for my colleagues and their families' members because I thought it was the right thing to do, I knew them and they were my friends. You have to keep in mind that, whatever you do in life is an experience or a lesson to be learnt, however, every man reap what he sow, therefore when you do good unto yourself and others, along the line you will be rewarded, on the other hand, if you take the law into your own hand, as though you made the rules, there is a price to pay, it doesn't matter who you are in this world, everything has a price good and bad.

Yes there are times my conscious bother me, because of decision I made for another human being life, it not easy to say get over it, mistakes has been made, in one or another lives, that you can erase, but mentally they will never go away, and this I must deal with the rest of my life, now or when the time comes for me to retire as being of Judge in the City of Ohio, I need to analyze the situation more carefully, these are peoples I am dealing with, you can just about say, their lives is in my hand.

So from this point on I going to take this matter into consideration, it is a job that I always wanted to do, the consequences that comes with the decision can be harsh, we all are part of this system.

Public Defendant

Danielle Staples

Let me tell you a little something about my background, which has me where I am today. My name is Danielle Staples, I am from Philadelphia, PA, I am four-five years of age no children's, nor have I ever been married. I came from a broken home with a younger brother, whom I had to look after when I was seven years old, my brother is fifteen years younger than me and mom she had her own thing going on and off, she was a part-time mother.

Most of my life, I raised my brother as my own child, most of the neighbors, thought he was my son, for a longtime until he went to Junior High School, so did Derrick, he would call me Mama Dee all of the time, as he gotten older, he now calls me Dee. I loved my brother, and I know he loves me as well, I believe this is why I never had children's of my own. I had to care for him and see that he finished school. Derrick was a good kid, he did not understand much about mother or her chaotic way of living, however she made it hard for us to have a normal life, at times, but in her own way she took care of the both of us.

She did her best, and I do not hold her accountable for her mistakes, what gives me the right to judge her or any other human being. The funny thing about this situation, we all makes mistakes, no one is perfect, yes mother did get me angry many times, but I would always think, by the grace of God there go I, we never know what is in front of us, each day that life brings us, one circumstances can change quicker than the blink of the eyes. As time went on Derrick went into the Navy he made a career in Computer Science, I explained to him the different issues that brought mother to her bottom. So he was okay in going away, and becoming a good son, brother and man.

THE HOUSE OF PUNISHMENT

Derrick, soon married and had twins sons, he still remained in the Navy, as a Captain and a teacher, in the State of Georgia, me I'm staying close to mother, she is a recovering addictive, and has come a long way staying clean, she does suffer a little with dementia, the good thing about this she no longer use drugs. Mother is sixty years of age, and I have to have someone look after her while I work at the Courthouse, I love my job and I would like to see the innocent have a fair trial, with so much going on, cases come in all day long. But I remain cool, calm and focus.

In some cases working with the defendant the odds can be greater, so I will do my best with the wisdom, knowledge and experience that I have in proceeding with the information submitted. There are so many cases I can talk about, but there is one case that really draws my attention to the matter, and I need all the time to sort this one out. This case will be brought to trial in two weeks, so I will take this time to think about it, pray, and plan that it has a successful ending.

PROSECUTOR

Malik August

Born and raised in Lakehurst, New Jersey with a family of great expectations, it was not easy to be myself. I was from a family of twelve and I consider myself the one that knew it all. I was the seventh child from the youngest, six brothers and five sisters. My father was a Judge for over forty years, and now is retired. My mom she was the principle at the public school, in NJ. Every one of my siblings has a very good position, in many careers, because my father saw to this.

My dad was very strict, with his children's and mom approved of his decisions, I guess she had no choice; after all he was a Judge of the Court. He was respected at home and on the job, even though, our dad was over protected of his children's every now and then I would dip and dap in and out of the street. I was very immature and hardhearted, I want to do what I wanted to do, and dad was not having this. My two older sisters, followed mother and worked in the school system as teachers, and my younger sister was a lawyers for license of inspection in NJ.

My other two middle sisters, worked in the courthouse as law clerks, I have two brothers who worked at City Hall in the zoning and permit department, two brother in the Service, Army and Marines, the other brothers one in construction and my youngest brother next to me he worked with politics. Everyone was doing their own things. I played around with my life for awhile, did not take things very seriously, I was young and thought I had time on my side.

Until one day I got myself into an altercation, with a few guys on the street, after this experience, and how my life flashed in front of my face, that scared me straight, I decided to go to college and major in law, I wanted to become a prosecutor. So I did, after finishing college, my dad got me a job in the system, he was well known, I did this for five years, and I feel in love with someone, who was visiting here on a conference for advertising pharmaceutical products for a company. We got really acquaintance with each other, and I decide in a few months I would move to Ohio to be with her. I would not have my family to depend on; I had to become a more responsible person, as well as a Prosecutor for the system.

So the time came and I left for Ohio I married, Vanessa and you know how the story goes, my family and friends were all there. A few weeks later I became a father to a baby girl. Being a Prosecutor for the system, it takes up a lot of your time, I became a family man, I do not know how my father did it, but I am never home, too spend enough time with my wife and daughter, I guess when I was younger, I did not realize that my dad was not there most of the time either. I love my wife and daughter, but I do not plan on having a family as big as my parents did, I have fifteen years in the system and I decided to do fifteen more years and retire, so that I can be a father and husband, that is one of the good example my dad taught me.

No matter what case I take and work on, being a Prosecutor, it sometimes makes you think whether the defendant is right, is he still considered wrong. I do have a conscience and, I would like to be just and fair, however the case, which I been assigned too, is in two weeks, a person accused of murder, so I am a little nervous, dealing with the Judge, Juror and the Public Defender, first time in the City of Ohio. This is going to be something to look forward to, so I will pray and have faith that this situation goes well. Preparing myself to continue to be good at what I do, hoping everything in the process, that the time, I spent in deciding working on this case whether the defendant is guilty or innocent.

ABOUT ADULTS

LET'S BE ADULTS ABOUT THIS
JUST STOP LOOK AND LISTEN, IT'S NOT LIKE I'M DISSIN, YOU AND ME, HE AND SHE.
IMAGINE A WORLD WHERE WE CAN BE FREE, FROM THE AGONY, LIVING RESPONSIBLY

LET'S BE ADULTS ABOUT THIS
WE NEED TO BE MORE ATTENTIVE TO THE NEEDS OF OUR SEEDS, SO THEY CAN BE ALL
THEY CAN BE, WITHOUT THE HELP OF THE ARMY

LET'S BE ADULTS ABOUT THIS
NO MORE GAMES, THE B.S IS CHILDS PLAY, I DON'T HAVE THE TIME, NOR THE DAY
WE CAN PLAY LATER WHEN WE BECOME GREATER,
PUT IN THE WORK NOW AND IGNORE THE HATERS, BECOME A HOMEOWNER, STOP BEING
A LONER, I WANT TO PAY ALL MY BILLS, SO I CAN UNWIND AND CHILL
TO BE ABLE TO RELAX AND FEEL AND DEAL WITH LIFE, THAT'S FOR REAL

LET'S BE ADULTS ABOUT THIS
CONFRONT EVERYTHING MOVIN, DON'T SIT BACK AND BEGIN CRUSIN, ITS LIFE TAKES IT
SERIOUS, LEAVE THE SUCKER ALONE BECAUSE THEY ARE DELIRIOUS
GET WITH THE WINNERS AND BECOME A WINNER, NOT WITH THE LOSERS AND GET THINNER
STREET LIFE IS ALWAYS RE-PLAYED, ANOTHER FOOL VOLUNTEERED TO GET SPRAYED

LET'S BE ADULTS ABOUT THIS
NETWORK WITH THE QUALIFIED, BUILD A FOUNDATION THAT'S UNIFIED
AT THE END OF THE ROAD, THE SACRIFICE WILL BE WORTH IT.
REMEMBER TO PUT IT DOWN, FLIP IT AND REVERSE IT.
DO IT RIGHT THIS TIME AROUND, PROMISE TO KEEP YOUR HEAD UP
NOT DOWN TO THE GROUND, STAND TALL AND PROUD, SCREAM OUT LOUD
YOU FINALLY MADE IT AS AN ADULT NOW; I'M AN ADULT ABOUT THIS

DESCRIPTION

To my readers, this book is based on true time and events,* the beginning is a summary of the author, it enlighten the good and bad times, of being raised in a large family environment. It also speaks of many situations and circumstances in which could have been done differently. The main character is a guy name Royale who thought he had much control over his life, it all started out to be pleasure and fun.

Royale was a very intelligent and caring being, however he got caught up in a situation that became totally powerless with no self-control. Royale is a scared and confused drug addict, who is now serving life in prison for a crime that, was committed, while under the influences of alcohol and drugs. This can become very dangerous, when not making the right choices it could have caused him his life. There are many other people who are involved in this story, such as the victims, the jury, judge, prosecutor, and the public defender, who all play a part in this detrimental, painful and touching story, which most readers will identify with the events of what has happen in these people's lives.

*Yes Royale is a victim of drug abuse, who is trying now to regain his life back, despite the wrong he have done, does he deserve another chance for a fair trial? Let's find out as we read **The House of Punishment**, the price of another life. You as the reader will enjoy this book; it is therapeutic, enjoyable, powerful messages, conflict, joy, forgiveness and much more inspiring words and poems.*

*Some names in this story have been changed.